D1469335

Sleep in Peace

Herald Press

Scottdale, Pennsylvania
Waterloo, Ontario

Ingrid Hess

Library of Congress Cataloging-in-Publication Data

Hess, Ingrid.
  Sleep in peace / Ingrid Hess.
     p. cm.
  ISBN 978-0-8361-9381-7 (pbk. : alk. paper)
  1. Children—Prayers and devotions—Juvenile literature.
  2. Bedtime prayers—Juvenile literature. I. Title.
  BV265.H47 2007
  242'.62—dc22
                                        2007011831

SLEEP IN PEACE
Copyright © 2007 by Herald Press, Scottdale, Pa. 15683
  Published simultaneously in Canada by Herald Press,
  Waterloo, Ont. N2L 6H7. All rights reserved
Library of Congress Catalog Card Number: 2007011831
International Standard Book Number: 978-0-8361-9381-7
Printed in the United States of America
Book and cover design by Ingrid Hess

12 11 10 09 08   10 9 8 7 6 5 4 3 2

To order or request information, please call
1-800-245-7894, or visit www.heraldpress.com.

to Susan

When the sun is setting
and the day is done,
when the world is quiet
and the night's begun

God loves you, sweet child.
Sleep in peace.

When the bustling day
of the city's through,
when it's bedtime for
many kids like you,

or when cows are in
and the barn's shut tight,
when your farm's asleep
for the rest of the night

God loves you, sweet child.
Sleep in peace.

When your games and toys
have been put away
and the playroom's quiet
til another day

God loves you, sweet child.
Sleep in peace.

When you're traveling late
far from your own bed,
when you're sleeping in
a new place instead

God loves you, sweet child.
Sleep in peace.

When bull frogs croak
and the lizards creep,
when your houseboat rocks
as you float to sleep

God loves you, sweet child.
Sleep in peace.

When atop a mountain
winter's cold winds blow,
when the land is covered
by a drift of snow

or when shadows lengthen
on the desert sand,
when the air turns chilly
and cools off the land

God loves you, sweet child.
Sleep in peace.

When you snuggle close
to keep cozy warm
as you hear the crash
of a thunderstorm

God loves you, sweet child.
Sleep in peace.

When you have some friends
sleeping nearby you,
when you share your pillows
and blankets too

God loves you, sweet child.
Sleep in peace.

When the night owls hoot
and their echoes soar
high above the trees
on the forest floor

God loves you, sweet child.
Sleep in peace.

When your hammock slowly
begins to sway
in the island breeze
at the end of the day

God loves you, sweet child.
Sleep in peace.

When you're keeping watch
over flocks of sheep
and it's finally time
for your turn to sleep

or when shadows dance
all around the fire,
when your eyes get heavy
and you start to tire

God loves you, sweet child.
Sleep in peace.

When the shining stars
and the street lamps' light
and the fireflies' glow
all light up the night

God loves you, sweet child.
Sleep in peace.

When the sky is dark
and the moon lights the way
as you head for home
at the end of the day

God loves you, sweet child.
Sleep in peace.

When the winter's chill
makes your cheeks turn red,
when you're headed off
to your cozy bed

God loves you, sweet child.
Sleep in peace.

When the songs you've sung
fill the evening sky
with the melody
of a lullaby

and when bedtime stories
have all been read,
when your memories
swirl inside your head

God loves you, sweet child.
Sleep in peace.

The Sleepy Moon

When you've had your bath
and your teeth are brushed,
when you're in your pajamas
and the house is hushed

God loves you, sweet child.
Sleep in peace.

When you've kissed good night
and the daylight ends,
when your house gets quiet
as the night descends

God loves you, sweet child.
Sleep in peace.

When your light is off
or your lantern's spark
is no longer bright
and your room is dark

when you've said your prayers
and you're tucked in tight
and it's time to dream
for the rest of the night

God loves you, sweet child.
Sleep in peace.

When the moon is high
and the stars are bright,
when you're fast asleep
and it's late at night

God loves you, sweet child.
Sleep in peace.

The Author & Illustrator

Ingrid Hess is a textbook designer for a large publisher in Chicago, and illustrates Timbrel, a magazine published by Mennonite Women. She is a graduate of Goshen College in Indiana, and trained in fine arts at Indiana University. Ingrid lives in Chicago and frequently volunteers for the fair-trade organization Ten Thousand Villages. In 2005, she illustrated Praying With Our Feet.